D0719210

For Mum and Dad, who made sure that
Father Christmas always found me

J.R.

For the amazing Barney, Joshua, John and Lydia
with love and thanks for being you

T.B.

First published in Great Britain in 2010 by
Gullane Children's Books
185 Fleet Street, London, EC4A 2HS
www.gullanebooks.com

1 3 5 7 9 10 8 6 4 2

A CIP record for this title is available from the British Library.

ISBN: 978-1-86233-802-9

Printed and bound in China

Ferdie's Christmas

Julia Rawlinson
illustrated by *Tiphanie Beeke*

It was an ice-bright Christmas Eve, and the sky was a dazzling blue. Every tree in the wood was frost-sprinkled and sparkling, and frozen puddles creaked and crackled under Ferdie's paws. He padded down the burrow-bank where the rabbits used to live, and bounced over the fallen tree that blocked their old front door.

And stopped. And looked.
And had a terrible thought. . .

"What are you doing?" asked Squirrel,
looking down from the branches.
"Making a trail to the rabbits' new burrow
for Father Christmas," said Ferdie.
"Otherwise they might not get their presents,"
gulped Squirrel, and he scampered down
to help Ferdie collect more sticks.

The trail passed between bare trees and crossed the tinkling, ice-rimmed stream, as the sun began to set, turning a dazzling gold. Ferdie and Squirrel shivered with cold and hurried up the little hill to where the mice were draping their nest with holly and ivy leaves.

"What are you doing?" asked the mice.

"We're making a trail,"
said Ferdie.

"To the rabbits' new
burrow," added Squirrel.

"For Father Christmas,"
added the birds.

"You'd better hurry,"
said the mice. "It's getting late.
We'll help you!"

So Ferdie, Squirrel, the birds and the mice finished the trail to the rabbits' new home, which was sweet with the smell of blackberry pie, cosy and warm. They gathered round the crackling fire, thawing out their icy noses, nibbling pieces of pie and singing Christmas songs. And while Squirrel put on a juggling show with holly berries and mistletoe, outside in the shivery darkness . . .

it began to snow.

Fat white flakes tumbled softly from a heavy sky.

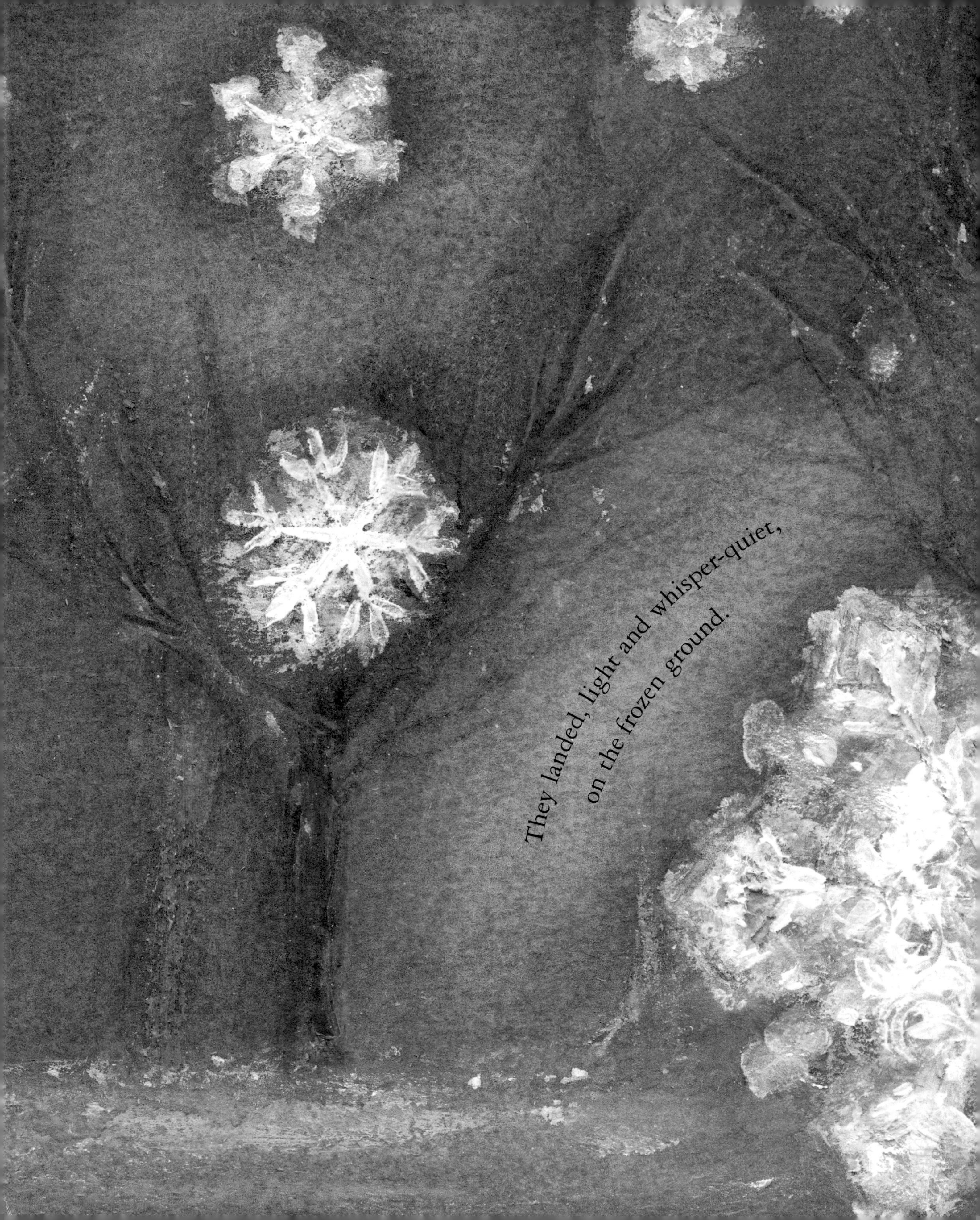

They landed, light and whisper-quiet,
on the frozen ground.

But curled in the cosy
hollow of an oak tree,
Squirrel began to snore.

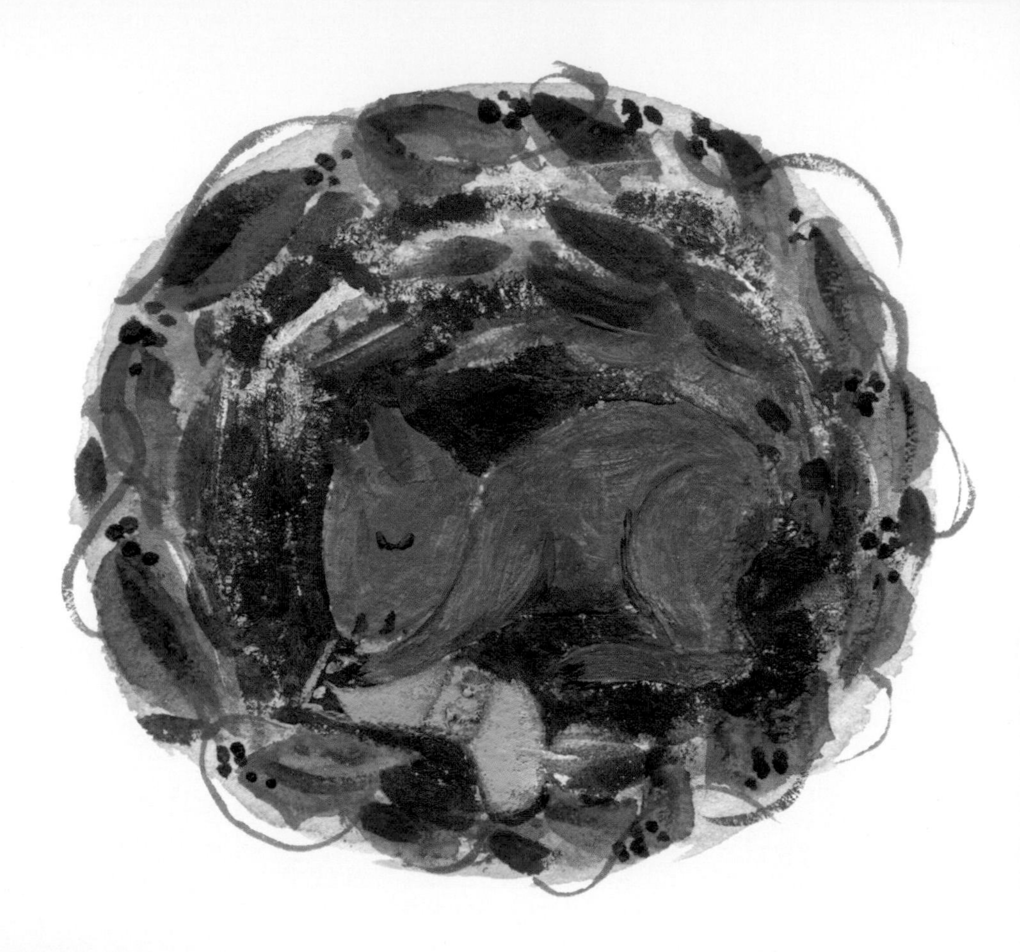

High in the snowy
branches of a fir tree,
the birds began to doze.

In their toasty warm nest,
the mice dreamt of
ribbon-wrapped berries.

And in his snug little bed,
Ferdie's eyes closed.

So when Father Christmas
came to call, everyone
was fast asleep. And next
morning, when Ferdie rushed
to the rabbits' burrow . . .

Father Christmas had found them after all!

"I'm sorry I went to sleep," puffed Ferdie,
"but I've brought you a Christmas rose."
"And we've brought nuts," panted Squirrel, pulling the mice through the snow.
"And we've brought berries," sang the birds, spiralling in the snow-bright sky.

“And best of all you’ve brought yourselves.
There’s room in the burrow for everyone . . .

". . . Happy Christmas!"

cried the rabbits, and they welcomed their friends into the berry-bright warmth of their home.